He closed the gap, his big h
denim encased thigh. "I prefe
know what they w

To all the rest of the world, Elizabeth Clarke had it all.
A successful husband. A beautiful home. And now a son off to
university.
She is a perfect housewife with the perfect life.
It's a lie.
Her husband is a lying, drinking philanderer who hates her as much
as she loathes him. Her home is beautiful, but empty, nothing more
than a gilded cage to keep her trapped in a world she never wanted.
That is, until he came back to town.
Hugh Becket.
Her son's best friend.
He's hot, young, and so forbidden.
Elizabeth knows she should stay away, but when the devil comes
knocking on her door in the middle of the night, what's a poor
neglected trophy wife to do?

**Forbidden Desire is a super hot older woman / younger man
romance. It has a HEA, NO Cliffhanger and all the steam you
have come to expect from the Lord of Lust.**

Forbidden Desire

Confessions of a Trophy Wife

Book 1

L.M. Mountford

L.M. Mountford
United Kingdom
Forbidden Desire
Confessions of a Trophy Wife
Book 1

Publisher's Note: This is a work of fiction. Names, characters, places, and incidents are a product of the author's imagination. Locales and public names are sometimes used for atmospheric purposes. Any resemblance to actual people, living or dead, or to businesses, companies, events, institutions, or locales is completely coincidental.

Edited by readabit: Copy Editing and Proofreading Services Est 2018

L.M. Mountford -- 1st Ed.
ISBN: 978-1-913945-25-1

ABOUT THE AUTHOR

A self-confessed Tiger fanatic, L.M. Mountford was born and raised in England, first in the town of Bridgewater, Somerset, before later moving to the city of Gloucester where he currently resides. A fully qualified and experienced Scuba Diver, he has travelled across Europe and Africa diving wrecks and seeing the wonders of the world.

Other Titles by L.M. Mountford

Collections
Deliciously Sinful Liaisons
Temptation and Seduction

The Sweet Temptations Series
The Babysitter
The Boss's Daughter

Just Friends Series
Just Once

Broken Heart Series
Broken

Confessions of a Trophy Wife
Forbidden Desire

Stand Alone Titles
Uncovered
Serving the Senator
Together in Sydney
Blood Lust
Training Tracey
Valentine Misadventures
Play Time

FORBIDDEN
Desire

CONFESSIONS OF A TROPHY WIFE
BOOK 1

THE LORD OF LUST
L.M. MOUNTFORD

Prologue

Watching her son drive down the road, Elizabeth Clarke sighed heavily.

Today should have been one of the happiest days of her life. He'd done it. After five years - five long years of waiting, procrastination and disappointment. He'd finally done it. Victor, her sweet baby boy, was finally moving out and going to university.

It hadn't been easy. He'd done abysmally in his GCSEs, barely scraping a passing grade, so he'd taken a break to work and save some money, before going out and blowing it under the guise of travelling. He'd wanted to find himself, he'd told her, see the world. And he had, from what she could gather. He'd seen the world, one club at a time.

She doubted she'd ever know what he'd gotten up to out there, and she didn't want to. He hadn't written or called, just turned up on the doorstep, then a few days later enrolled in the city college for various courses. He'd worked hard, gotten his head down, studied, and finally, he had done it.

She should have been ecstatic, proud and practically bouncing off the walls. What mother wouldn't be?

Yet all Elizabeth felt was a sense of abandonment. He was going, leaving her all alone with…

Him.

The thought sent a shiver down her spine that had nothing to do with the autumn breeze whispering through her long raven hair.

When the car turned around the street's bend, time seemed to hold its breath and Elizabeth wanted so badly to bend the laws of space and time around that moment, that last glimpse of her son, and stretch it on for an eternity. Then he was gone and who knew when she would see him again.

Of course, deep, deep down, she knew she was being silly. Oxford wasn't exactly Beirut. Victor was just a few hours' drive away. Close enough that he could come home for every Sunday roast.

And go back after.

That bitter pill drove her back indoors.

Desperate to keep busy, she set about doing the one job that had always proved as a source of comfort to her - cleaning. There was usually so much she needed to do, so many jobs that had to be done. A household of a young adult male was one that never stayed clean and required constant attention. Unfortunately, there was now a very vital part of that equation, which was no longer prevalent in her life. Without which it no longer felt like home. Without Victor, it was just another immaculate showroom, a haunted residence for a lingering spirit, the ghost of a neat and impeccable mother, and the basecamp of her travelling salesman husband.

Elizabeth furrowed her brow with disgust as she looked upon the neat pile of stacked plates and dishes in her cupboard, laundry ironed and folded away, and practically sparkling worktops. Then she felt her stomach tighten.

How could it be? Was there something she had forgotten, no that couldn't be it. She had followed the same routine she had always done and yet, somehow, she had finished five hours' worth of work in less than half an hour.

With a dispirited sigh, she walked across her now impeccably clean kitchen and fell into one of her dining table chairs. Resting her head in her hands, she tried to think of something, anything, to do.

God, how had her life come to this?

Patrick, he was why. That bastard had always been the source of her misery.

In school she'd always been outgoing, adventurous, the popular girl, always doing something. Be it tennis training or dance classes, going out with friends or babysitting the neighbourhood's kids - anything that would get her out of the house.

Then Patrick had entered her life and less than five months after her eighteenth birthday they were married.

He'd been so handsome then. They'd made a lovely photo couple. The strapping rugby captain, all muscle and easy smiles, with the leggy athletic beauty on his arm in flowing white lace. The gown had been a work of art. It took a lot of looking in the photos to see the bump, the memento of a night she could remember only as an alcoholic haze, but that would prove to completely reshape her life.

It had been a small ceremony for family and friends. Then he'd promptly whisked her across to the small house his parents had bought them on the over-side of the county, near where Somerset met Devonshire in one of the areas of many sleepy little villages. Ideally located for Victor's new role in the family business, but far away from her friends and family.

So, she'd become a mother and a housewife. The iconic role reversal from party girl and athlete to domestic goddess.

And she'd revelled in it, the challenge of being a new mother, the thrill of bringing life into the world.

For Patrick however, the switch had come as a nasty shock.

The walking, talking definition of a good time Charlie, his family had set him up in a role he'd been born to, salesman for their peat factory. And if the idea of going from garden centre to garden centre, sweet talking them into buying his family's products, hadn't quite lived up to the fast-talking rugby star's dreams of adult life, then he certainly hadn't bargained on all his hard work going to support his wife and child.

Or that he'd have to keep it in his pants.

She gave a dry laugh at the notion, before her eyes suddenly lit up.

Jennifer!

CHAPTER
1

Years ago, the road had been a quiet snaking stretch
of tarmac, but back in 1993, work had begun on a
site that would become one of the UK's largest shopping
outlet villages. In less than a year, Clarke's Village had
transformed the A-39 into a bustling thoroughfare that
during rush hour could be lined with bumper-to-bumper
congestion. At ten in the morning, however, when all the rest
of the world was being swept up in the ebb and flow of
everyday life, there was very little in the way of traffic.

Sleek and polished to a high shine, the electric blue
Audi TT convertible sped along the snaking stretch of single-
lane tarmac. Heedless of the rain pelting the windscreen,
Elizabeth kept her foot to the floor, relishing in the sweet rush
of adrenaline as she sped through the numerous villages
dotting the A-39.

She loved driving.

Fast driving was like great sex. It was freedom, a
complete surrender to the moment. Behind the wheel, she
forgot the disappointments, forgot the broken dreams, her

sham of a marriage. She forgot all the downslopes her life had taken. There was only the road, the rush, and the sexy throb of the engine purring through her. It was her escape.

There was no warning for the turning, just a sudden gaping maw in the surrounding woodland as the tarmac branched off. Used to the turn, Elizabeth dropped a gear and dragged the wheel around, adding just a dab of brake as the TT swung gracefully round the hairpin, then corrected for the straight and sped on. It was a reckless manoeuvre, stupid even in the rain along such a treacherous blind turn, but the momentary, stomach flipping rush made the risks seem rather insignificant.

Of course, she never had much to worry about in her Audi. The TT responded to her every command like the fine German engineered automobile it was.

Which was good, because off of the A-39, the way became a snaking lane of old tarmac and blind turns behind any number of which could await the hulk of an oncoming tractor or bus.

She floored it, and the Audi turned from a purring kitten to a raging tiger. It roared and kept roaring until she pulled into the familiar L-shaped driveway of *Forbidden Fruit* Cottage.

Despite its name, *Forbidden Fruit* Cottage was, in fact, a bungalow. A stately bungalow, with numerous extensions, two conservatories and three acres of private land. It also happened to be the only property within two miles.

Heedless of the rain, Elizabeth got out of the sports car and sauntered up to the front door. Overhead, the sky was dark and subdued, the sun blotted out by the canopy of thick grey clouds. The rain that had been a mere trickle when she set off, fell in a continuous sheet that drenched her from head to toe in the few strides to the front step.

All too aware of the icy rivulets running down the back of her neck, she raised a hand to knock, only for the door of heavy English oak, painted a deep blue with a plaque stamped *Forbidden Fruit*, to suddenly swing inward.

Elizabeth felt her breath catch.

Oh my…

CHAPTER
2

// Well, this is certainly a pleasant surprise. Hello
there, Mrs Clarke." Hugh Becket could barely keep
his grin at bay as he opened the door.

Damn, she's still so fucking gorgeous.

"Oh…" Elizabeth had the deer in headlights look as she
took him in. "Ugh, hi Hugh, is your mum in?"

"I'm afraid you just missed her. She and the old man
have flown south for the winter and left me here to mind the
fort." As he spoke, he eyed her hungrily, giving her a slow
once over, then another for good measure. "You look good."

She always had.

"Thanks … err you mind letting me in? It's pissing it
down out here. I'm getting soaked."

Good to know.

"Sure, I'll get you a towel." He stepped aside to let her
pass, his eyes dropping down to admire her backside as she
passed. It took a feat of Herculean endurance for him not to
whistle. Drenched as they were, her already skinny jeans
moulded to her deliciously curved backside like a second

skin. And that spaghetti top didn't exactly leave much to the imagination, either.

Suddenly very aware of the erection straining against the front of his own jeans, he pulled the door shut and wheeled around to the airing cupboard. There, he busied himself with rummaging through the ample assortment of towels on the shelves, careful to take just long enough for the very prominent bulge to diminish, for the most part anyway. However, the task was made all the more difficult by the fact he could practically feel her eyes now travelling over him.

It was only when he was certain she would be growing suspicious by his prolonged search that he reluctantly turned back and handed her a fluffy pink towel. At the time, though her eyes were already a little further south and they seemed to grow two sizes too big when they fixed on his groin. Which, in turn, responded to the attention.

Oh … shit.

"Can I get you anything? Tea? Coffee?" Hugh quickly asked, careful to keep his voice level even as she openly ogled him for a moment before dragging her eyes away.

"Err tea, please, I could murder a brew." With that she snatched the towel and fled into the living room.

Oh God, was that monster his cock or did he just stick a bloody cucumber down his trousers?

Furiously scrubbing her hair with the towel, Elizabeth felt her cheeks burning at the memory of the appendage straining against Hugh's trousers.

Oh fuck, he's huge … Did I do that to him?

The thought came out of nowhere and sent a pulse of heat straight down to her clit. Shocked, she immediately tried to brush it aside, but then couldn't help remembering the way he'd been watching her, the hot predatory gleam in his eyes as he'd looked her over.

She knew that look. It was a hot look, dark and hungry. Sultry and very, very dangerous in the eyes of a young stud.

She'd seen it a lot when she was younger. On Saturday nights out when she went out to hit the town with her girlfriends. The clubs and bars would be thronged with packs of men who'd watch them with that same look. Like packs of wild dogs, eyeing up a fresh juicy bit of meat. Some of Patrick's mates had given her that same look over the years too, when they'd had a few too many and were likely to get handsy...

But to see Hugh giving her that same look. No, it couldn't be.

She'd known him and his mother for years, since he and Victor were kids in playschool. He was young enough to be her son. He was her friend's son, and her own son's best friend. And she was too old for him, much too old.

I'm old enough to be his mother.

"Tea's up!"

Her heart leapt at the husky voice.

Aimlessly scrubbing her hair, she swung around to find Hugh standing in the doorway, holding two steaming mugs. The vision was as breath-taking as it had been when he had been standing in the doorway. The image of him, in those casual *distressed* jeans and tight shirt, radiating such raw masculinity, an alpha male at ease in his territory, made her long to be twenty years younger.

He placed them on the coffee table.

"Still lots of milk and three sugars, right?"

Placing the towel over the headrest of one of the two matching armchairs that encircled one side of the table, she sat in one corner of the sofa that sat opposite. Able to practically feel the heat of his eyes on her skin through her clothes, she picked up the mug and sipped. Sweet and just that little bit shy of hot. Perfect.

"Cheers." Elizabeth sipped and sipped, until she knew she couldn't avoid talking to Hugh any longer without seeming rude. Then she mentally kicked herself. She was being ridiculous.

This was Hugh, just Hugh. It didn't matter that he had grown into a smouldering and sexy-as-hell Adonis. It was still Hugh. She focused on that, trying to think of the little boy she'd use to watch play in the park.

"So, Jen and Mike took off to the sun and gave you run of the house, huh? Where'd they go?"

"Gran Canaria," he answered, sitting beside her. As it was a two-seater, there was just enough room on the sofa for them both. Just. "Dad scored a big commission, so they rented a condo out there for the month to celebrate."

"Lucky for some..." Elizabeth could feel herself shaking from his closeness. His tone was offhand and casual, but the way the smokiness of his voice curled around the words, he might as well have been whispering dirty fuck-me-talk right in her ear. "So, does this mean you've finished your pupillage?"

He picked his own mug up off the glass tabletop. "Yep, I'm now a fully certified and experienced lawyer."

"That's great." Her breath caught as he drank, her eyes immediately fixing on the subtle movements of his throat as he swallowed. Then she noticed his eyes, those intense, baleful blue eyes, burning bright against the inky dark of his pupils, watching her over the rim. She quickly looked away. "What are you going to do now? Take a break here while your parents are away then head off back to the city? Get snapped up by some big firm and become a hotshot city lawyer? I could just see you in the Old Bailey. Parading around in your robe and wig, then hitting the streets with your expensive tailored suits and flash super car. You were always a flash git, even when you and Victor were kids."

"Ouch," he mocked a hurt look. Then, putting the mug down, he rounded on her, the force of his presence enough to have her edging back into the sofa. "No, actually I'm here to stay. I took a job with a small firm down in Taunton. And I'm not involved in criminal law. I handle insurance."

"Insurance?"

"Yeah, insurance, and a bit of property law. It's less glamorous but steadier." As he spoke, Elizabeth couldn't help noticing he was edging closer. "And my clients aren't likely to throw acid in my face if I can't get them off."

Their growing proximity had awareness tingling through her arms, and heat gathering in the pit of her belly. "Fair point. So, you've just moved back into your old room? Aren't you a bit … err *big* for that now?"

"A little." He teased and actually winked at her. "That's why I'm kipping in the spare room while I look for a place of my own."

"To rent?"

"Afraid so."

He was getting closer, too close.

"Well it shouldn't take long to find somewhere, if you know where to look. You know, there are some very nice places over my way." Fuck, why had she said that.

"I *remember*." His voice lowered, growing hotter like the space between them. "You'll have to show me around, give me the grand tour."

In spite of herself, Elizabeth's heart leapt at the idea.

"Sure, pop round anytime you're free and I'd be happy to show you the neighbourhood." God, what was she saying? She really needed to stop talking now. But she couldn't stop herself, it had just come out as her mind swam with the thought of him and her, alone, that body pushing up against her, all hard and male, his wicked mouth doing unspeakable things.

No, this wasn't good. She needed to get things onto a safer ground. "I know Victor would love it. You haven't seen him in ages. And it's such a great place to start a family, I'm sure your girlfriend will love it."

He smirked, as if he could see how close she was to snapping. And revelled in it. "Well, that sounds great, all I need to do now is to find a wife."

"Oh, so there's no one…"

"Oh, there's someone," he said. "There has been for a long time. She just doesn't know it, *yet*."

Elizabeth felt a lump developing in her throat, her heart racing like a bird in a cage. "Well, I'm sure she's a very special girl."

"She is, but I'm not really interested in girls." He closed the gap, his big hand moving to gently rest on her denim encased thigh. "I prefer more mature women. Women who know what they want and how to get it."

She wanted him.

Wanted to touch him, taste him, bite him.

Wanted to lick her way down those delicious abs, tear those damn jeans off with her teeth, and suck his big fucking cock until-

He kissed her hungrily, all heat and instinct.

CHAPTER
3

She gasped, a soft whimper of protest, as the feeling of his lips crushing against hers set every nerve in her alive, but she didn't pull away. She didn't resist as his tongue danced across the roof of her mouth, ravishing her with lush licks that made her toes curl before entangling with hers. Nor did she try and escape when his powerful hands enveloped her, cupping her buttocks with exquisite force and dragging her across so his resurrected cock pushed against the throbbing heat at her centre.

Then she was straddling his lap, the softness of his hair tickling the skin between her fingers as she fisted it and kissed him back, and nothing seemed to matter.

She didn't know what she was doing, but suddenly she didn't care.

She didn't care that it was wrong. Didn't care that he was her son's best friend. Didn't care that he was half her age.

She didn't care that she was a married woman.

He was just too much, too much for her to resist, to deny.

Hugh groaned a low throaty sound when she began to suck his tongue, the throbbing purr tingling down her spine to spike in her clit as his fingers squeezed her bum, crushing her to him. The sting and his roughness turned her on all the more. Fuck, she'd forgotten how good this could feel.

How good it should feel.

It had been so long since a man had made her feel like this, she couldn't help her little squeak of protest when he pulled away. Even so, A part of her screamed that it was for the best. They couldn't do this, it was wrong, it was so very bad…

"Hugh!" His name left her in a hot breathy moan as his lips covered that sensitive spot behind her ear and sucked.

She couldn't believe what was happening. What she was doing.

It was so surreal, like she was waking from a dream but not quite, trapped in that void where dreams met reality.

She didn't do this. She'd never done anything like this.

But she'd wanted to. Fantasised about it. Dreamt about it, but never…

Heat, want, and greed surged through her as tingling sensations zapped through her from her head to the tips of her fingers and toes. Moans poured from her, hot and wanton. Somewhere in the back of her subconscious, she just registered the weight of his desire pushing against the heat throbbing in the cradle of her hips. The idea that she was affecting this young stud as potently as he was her, was so exciting, she couldn't resist. She needed to touch him, feel him.

Her hands moved slowly, cautiously, almost ridiculously so, given their predicament. However, she couldn't help it, half afraid the lightest touch, too bold, might shatter the spell and repulse him.

So, Elizabeth clung to him, her body crushed to his, hands pawing at his back through his shirt. He felt so hard.

Not bulky the way bodybuilders strived for, but solid, corded and toned. A slab of marble chiselled layer by layer into a work of art. Michael Angelo's *David* given life.

At any other moment, she might have wondered how the devil he had managed it, while at the same time juggling the hectic life of a lawyer in training. However now, all she wanted was to see him, feel his skin and worship him. If only his bloody shirt wasn't tucked so neatly into his jeans, barring her from immediate access. It just wasn't fair. It would take too long for her to pull it loose, and the act itself presented the considerable problem of having to take her hands off him.

Worse still, Hugh was faster, and bolder. Much bolder.

While his mouth worked her into a frenzy, ravishing her sensible tendons with licks and nips, one of his hands worked its way up beneath her top. It was cold against her heated skin, but the chill only added to the sensuousness of his touch. His fingers brushed over her naked flesh, up her midriff, over her ribs, gathering up the hem of her top as it went. He was careful to avoid her breasts however, and neglect made her nipples ache as the garment was pushed up and over her bountiful cleavage...

He left the spaghetti-string top there, bunched and rolled up under her arms. With a final nip of her earlobe, he pulled back to admire his handiwork. In a dark, far flung corner of her mind that was still capable of rational thought, a voice urged her to come to her senses. To slap that smug look off his gorgeous face and cover herself.

It was quickly pushed aside however, when she saw the look in his eyes as he took her in. How long had it been since Patrick had looked at her like that? Had he ever?

He rumbled an approving purr. Deep and low, it thrummed through his body into hers wherever their skin touched, making her sex clench. Clearly, he liked what he saw, and the thought made her glad she'd worn the red lace bra adorned with black filigree.

It was a tad too expensive and ornate to ever be considered practical, but the way it pushed her tits up and lifted the years, made the expense a thing of little account.

Her ass also happened to look great in the matching thong, if she did say so herself.

"Mmm … your tits are amazing."

His words thrummed through her, straight down to her pulsing clit, as the pad of his thumb brushed brazenly over her breasts. Teasing around her bra. Just inches from where she needed it.

"You know I used to dream about fucking them when I was younger. I'd jerk off thinking about burying my cock in them while that mouth sucked me off, but what really made me blow was thinking about them bouncing while I fucked you. Especially when I went balls deep and you begged me to give it to you, to take your creamy cunt…"

Her breath came in short gasps that were only slightly due to the way he was starting to plump her cleavage, that huge palm rubbing over her nipple through the lace in the most exquisite torture. His dirty words were a seduction in their own right. The thought of him stroking that monster while he dreamed of having his way with her. It was more than she could stand.

No man had ever treated her like this. He was rough and knew what he wanted, knew what she wanted, even if she didn't know it. He made her feel. Made her lose herself in the moment. She couldn't think. She couldn't remember why she was there, or where she was, or even what had brought her to this sofa, with this stranger.

This wasn't the boy she'd known.

That boy had grown up. Become a man. A man who took what he wanted.

And he wanted her.

Wanted her so lustily, he ripped the bra away like it was dental floss. With a flick of his wrist, he discarded the expensive piece of lingerie, banished it to a place out of sight. Then the damp, delicious heat of his mouth replaced it, sucking in her nipple, making her gasp ragged breaths.

"Oh god, what … what are you doing to me…" she panted, her back arching as he brought his other hand up to cup and knead her neglected tit. Sparks and starbursts sizzled through her as he worshipped her breasts. Then abruptly, he switched, and his fingers rolled her slick right bud into a heightened state of arousal while his tongue swirled around and around her left in ever shrinking circles, until she just wanted to scream.

Somehow, Hugh knew just how to play her body like a fiddle.

Grabbing and squeezing, biting and sucking, rolling and pinching her nipples, he made her feel things…

Feel like a woman again. Made her feel all the things she'd forgotten in her years of captivity, her years of bondage, in matrimony. Bound to a weak, whimpering sham of a man

Made her feel that feeling again. That slick heat throbbing so insistently down in her centre. The delicious friction that accompanied it every time she moved.

He made her feel things, and she wanted more.

"Mmm … Yeah … that's it … fuck … you bad boy!"

The words were out before she really knew what she was saying. Almost by their own volition, her hands had threaded through his hair, both pulling him to her, and steadying her as she ground her body into his.

And suddenly Elizabeth's whole world was focused on that feeling.

The feeling of him sliding along her folds, through the layers of lace and denim, grinding against her clit.

God! He feels even bigger than he looks…

The feeling brought the whole world crashing down around her.

This wasn't right.

She couldn't do this.

She didn't do... this.

She was a respectable woman, a married woman. She didn't have random quickies with men half her age. She didn't shag strange men, even if they were the embodiment of a fucking sex god!

No, she wouldn't. She couldn't ... she ... she ... No ... No...

"No!"

In other circumstances, the look of stunned disbelief on Hugh's face as he jumped back would have looked rather comical. However, Elizabeth was in too much of a rush to appreciate it.

"I'm ... sorry ... that ... that was a mistake. I should ... I shouldn't have done that." Scrambling back, off of the sofa and to her feet, she pushed her top down, being careful to walk around the coffee table and put as much space between her and her ravisher as possible as she did.

Then without waiting for his reply, she was out of the room, down the hall, through the door, in her car and gone.

CHAPTER
4

Back home, in the safety of her kitchen, Elizabeth could barely keep her hands from shaking as she sipped her tea. The residual arousal clawed at her, thrumming her nerves like taught guitar strings.

The tea took the edge off, a little.

"God! What was that?"

She couldn't believe what she'd done. And with Hugh of all people.

It was like something out of a bloody porno. Throwing herself at a hot stud after seeing he had a big cock. All that was missing was the delivery man with a funny accent and the big sausage pizza.

Oddly though, she didn't feel the least bit guilty. Frustrated, sure. Disappointed, maybe. Horny, fuck yeah! But no guilt.

Why would she? Patrick had his indiscretions, his little playthings, his... *whores!*

So what if she had a little slip with a dark and dashing toy-boy. She was a woman, she had needs.

But to do it, or nearly do it, with Hugh!

Her friend's son. Hell, he was her own son's friend, and not just any friend, his best friend. He was as off limits as it got. And all the hotter for it.

She quickly chugged her drink, desperate to quell the memory of his hands on her, the searing heat of his touch sizzling across her skin, working its way too – *No!*

Damn it all to hell, she needed to get laid. That would get it all out of her system. How long had it been anyway, two months? Three? Yes, she needed to get fucked, that was all. She needed…

She paused, an idea lurching to mind and she looked to the kitchen window. The sky overhead was still grey and overcast, growing darker by the second as dusk crept in, but the rain was stopping.

Her lips broke into a sly smile when her gaze landed on the large and luxurious hot tub on the back porch.

Keeping his foot down hard on the accelerator, Hugh turned off the Bridgwater Road and sped down the residential street towards the Clarke family's household on the outskirts of the Bampton area. A glance at his Omega told him it was a little after eight. *Not much further now…*

He didn't know what he was going to say, but he just couldn't leave things standing with Elizabeth the way they were. It felt like he'd been waiting his whole life to have a chance with Elizabeth Clarke, and now that he'd tasted her, he wasn't about to let her get away.

Not now, not after he'd waited for so long.

Heedless of the rain pounding his windscreen, he sped his BMW M5 down the residential streets, taking the swerving bends lined by detached red brick and grey stone homes like turns on the Nürburgring.

The years of going to and from Mrs Clarke's house with his mum had drilled the route into his memory, but it had been a while. He almost thought he'd gone too far until he spotted Elizabeth's Audi and pulled in behind it on the drive.

Most of the ground floor lights in the house were on but, much to his delight, there was no sign of Mr Clarke's Alfa Romeo 4C. The old git might have complicated things, but if he was away on one of his infamous *business* trips, then his wife would be all alone.

And if her performance in his parent's living room was any indication, she was in desperate need of a little TLC. Well, maybe a little less T and a whole lot of L.

Shutting the quietly purring BMW down, he slid out of the driver's seat, pocketed the fob, and walked up the drive to the front door. His mouth suddenly drier than the desert, he tapped his knuckles against the painted timbers of the front door.

Against the soft patter of the rain, the knocks echoed like the blasts of a cannon. Suddenly nervous, Hugh couldn't help brushing himself down, trying to smooth his clothes as he awaited an answer.

None came.

He knocked again, a little harder this time. Still no answer.

Okay, time for Plan B.

There was a time when he and Victor knew all the secret ways in and out of each other's homes. Now the memories came swimming back. Dropping down into a crouch, he slinked round the edge of the building, beneath the overhanging ledge of the family room's window seat, and through the flower beds. The fake rock was exactly where he remembered, nestled into the roots of a stump that had once been a towering apple tree.

Retrieving the key, he rose up and moved around to the side of the house and unlocked the padlock securing the ornate iron side gate, between the house and the garage.

A quick open-palmed push had the gate swinging open with a low creak that practically screamed his presence to the world. Someone obviously hadn't been keeping on top of the building maintenance.

The alleyway between the two buildings leading to the back garden was inky black all the way to the steps of the back porch but he could hear commotion up ahead. A sound like water bubbling on the hob.

There was something else too, something softer, almost indistinguishable from the background, but that made his dick instinctively stir to life. He couldn't believe his luck. Heart hammering excitedly in his chest, he followed the sounds and edging forward, slowly peered around the edge.

Elizabeth was in her hot tub, her head propped on a rolled towel beside an almost empty wine glass. It was a very deep model, more than half sunken into the porch yet the steaming, bubbling water came all the way up to her shoulders. Nonetheless, the tops of her breasts were clearly visible as, eyes closed and biting her lip, she arched her back, her left hand fondling her cleavage.

In the soft golden hue of the back-porch light, it was obvious she had forgone a swimsuit.

Hugh greedily drank in the view. He'd been dreaming of this moment, picturing it ever since he first started noticing girls, no, since he'd started to notice women. He'd never been really interested in girls. They were always so prissy and uptight, or always playing games. They didn't know what they wanted or how to satisfy a man. And while their bodies were fun to play with, they could never compare to the lush full curves of a mature woman.

Mrs Clarke was the very epitome of a mature, beautiful woman.

His fantasy.

His goddess.

Patrick, that son of a bitch, didn't deserve her. He'd neglected and abandoned her, so tonight, Hugh would make her his.

He could just hear her panting, soft wanton moans. They were music to his ears and almost without realising what he was doing, his free hand began fumbling with the button of his far too tight trousers. He could scarcely breathe for the tightness. He had to be set free, to relieve the tension building in his groin...

"Mmm..." she purred, hot and breathy. "Fuck … Yes … give me that cock … oh-my-god … I need it, yes…"

Nearly tearing his trousers open, he grabbed his cock. He couldn't see her other hand, but he didn't need to. He could picture her fingering her slick wet pussy, working herself up, first one, then two fingers, her hips rolling and growing more urgent as she got closer. He matched her pace, pumping his cock, the shaft slick with precum, and greedily devoured the sight of her playing with her dusky pink nipple. Twisting and tugging, imitating the very treatment he'd given it just hours earlier.

He answered her low moans by thrusting himself into the tight coil of his fist. Still pent up from their earlier encounter, Hugh knew he wouldn't last long, and though he'd seen his share of pornography, this was the first time he'd ever watched a woman masturbate in real life. It was the most erotic thing he'd ever seen.

Porn was cheap titillation. Sex manufactured with all the passion and intensity stripped away, like Ikea flat pack furniture.

Once you'd seen one, you'd seen them all.

This was anything but cheap titillation. This was seduction. Hugh would never get tired of watching her.

She was a living woman, repressed and denied. A font of pent up sexual tension just starting to bubble to the surface and in desperate need of a good, hard-

"Oh God … that's it baby … pound that pussy … oh god … I'm gonna- fuck, I'm cumming, I'm cumming … Hugh!"

Oh shit!

He froze, his fist tight just under the head, the sound of her calling out his name in that ragged breathy voice, triggered a chain reaction that pushed him over the edge.

He came hard, shooting a thick stream of cum that arced into the darkness. Yet his eyes never strayed from the view of Elizabeth as her own climax ripped through her.

The orgasm she'd reached while thinking of him…

CHAPTER
5

Elizabeth had never expected to be doing this. She'd only wanted a soak in the hot tub, but then everything had spiralled out of control.

Her idea had worked.

As she lay soaking in the hot water, all her tension had just seemed to melt away and she was content to do nothing more than let the jets work their magic, carrying her away, back to that sofa in Jennifer's living room.

Hugh was with her, above her, topless with his jeans hanging low on his hips.

He was kissing her again, hot and hungry kisses. She could feel his desire for her burning strong and pressing demandingly between her thighs as he rolled his hips.

Sinking deeper into her fantasy, heat that had nothing to do with the hot tub spiralled around her belly. A long sigh passed her lips as her hands began to mirror her fantasy. Already stiff, her nipples tingled as her fingers teased around them and sensation rippled down her spine in a rush that had her cupping and squeezing her heavy bosom while her other palm moved down her belly.

"Mmm …Oh yes, you're such a bad boy…"

Hugh laid her down across the sofa, his hands ripping the clothes from their bodies. Then he was covering her, and she could barely keep from drooling as he took himself in hand, stroking from base to tip so that a milky drop appeared.

She wanted to lick it, taste it. No, taste him, and more. So much more. Only he was faster…

She moaned, biting her lip in pleasure as the feeling of a finger sliding through her sent a white-hot shiver of delight coursing through her centre. It was a poor substitute for a real cock, but she'd missed the feeling of having something inside her for so long that she hardly cared and began rocking against the invading digit.

"Fuck … Yes... give me that cock … oh-my-god … I need it, yes…"

Oh god, what was wrong with her?

It had never been like this, even in those years after Victor was born and Patrick had started spending more and more time away on business trips. She had kept her composure and forewent the sexual urges. Life had been simpler back then. Her days had been full, the nights lonely, but she had been too preoccupied with her role of being a young mother to give much thought to her neglected libido.

Now, however, things were different. Victor was away at university. She was alone, and what she had once thought insignificant, was resurfacing with a vengeance.

She was shaking, every nerve in her body tingling with sensations as she used her thumb to play with her clit while working two fingers in and out. Almost mindless with the clawing need to cum, her body tensed under the duress of hot waves and she moaned again, only louder, not caring who heard as she came for the first time in longer than she could remember.

God, how had she gone without a man for so long?

Then, as the waves receded and afterglow settled, she felt it.

It was only a momentary distraction. A prickling sensation of awareness that tickled the back of her neck and tingled through her skin, but it was enough.

Someone was watching her.

The thought had her on instant alert, the vulnerability of her position, and the repercussions of what she had been doing, suddenly blaringly oblivious. Nervously, she looked up and around at the upper windows of the homes that encircled her back garden. They were all dark behind the drawn curtains and blinds, however that did not distract her from the certainty that someone was out there.

She could feel their eyes on her and strangely, rather than feeling violated by the intrusion, it was turning her on all over again. The idea that someone she couldn't see was watching her through the gloom thrilled her, made her belly flutter and core pulse excitedly. It was such an exciting feeling, she was almost tempted to give her audience an encore.

God, when had she become such an exhibitionist?

From his hideaway, Hugh had a near perfect view of Elizabeth rising up out of the hot tub and towelling herself dry. She seemed to be taking her time and spent much more time than necessary patting away every lingering drop of water before wrapping the towel around herself and hurrying back into the house.

All right genius, what now?

Tucking his still-stiff erection back into his trousers, he glanced back down the pathway. He could go back the way he'd come and try the front door again. She would hear him this time and answer, but then what would he say? He hadn't given the matter any thought on the drive over, and after what he'd just witnessed, he'd probably be as tongue tied as a virgin on a date with Madison Ivy.

Or he could go home, think on the matter a little bit, then come back in the morning, after she'd…

After she'd what? Calmed down? He dismissed the notion immediately. He wouldn't go back, not now. He'd waited too long for this chance, he couldn't, he wouldn't, he…

He wheeled around, crossed the garden and stormed up the porch to the back door. Knowing it was unlocked, he twisted the knob and pushed the door open.

Elizabeth stood with her back to him, her towel replaced by a black silk dressing gown that barely covered her lush derriere. He could hear her humming a low melody as she busied herself with fastening the belt around her waist. Unable to resist the opportunity, he crossed the kitchen in quick strides and reached out a hand to cup her arse.

Totally oblivious to his presence, Elizabeth shrieked and whirled around, her eyes widening at the sight of him.

"Hugh! What are you-"

Her reprimand quickly died as he seized her lips with his, silencing her with a deep kiss. For one harrowing moment she tried to break free, wriggling and squirming and pushing against the solid mass enveloping her. However, his strong hands held her close, crushing her to him. Then his tongue swept past her lips, and the fight left her completely.

He felt her relax and he urged her back, big hands squeezing her butt then hoisting her up onto the counter.

There were no words or gestures. No explanations given or required.

His need for her was like an all-consuming fire in his blood, a raging inferno that would not be sated until he had devoured every bit of her. With a mind to do just that, he took advantage of his new leverage to deepen the kiss, their tongues becoming locked in an intimate dance that had them both panting with passion as he moved in between her splayed thighs.

Her hands were braced against his torso, urgently pushing his jacket down his arms before moving up to bury themselves in his hair. Their hips were rolling together in synchronised motions and they wantonly devoured one another until the need for oxygen forced Elizabeth to pull away. However, Hugh was not so easily deterred and trailed kisses along her jaw before bending down to nip along her neck, making her gasp and moan in undisguised delight. "Oh God … No … We can't … we shou-oh!"

Her protestations were weak and lacked any conviction when spoken amidst such needy tones. Paying them no heed, he crouched down between her thighs and hitched her long legs over his shoulders. She didn't fight him and he turned his eyes up to hold her gaze as he dipped his head.

Elizabeth couldn't believe what was happening.

Everything was going so fast. One minute she was just wondering what she should do for dinner. The next she was being hoisted atop her kitchen cabinets, watching Hugh's gorgeous chiselled face going down between her legs.

It was a scene taken straight out of her fantasies and when his tongue flicked over her still oversensitive clit, she completely forgot all of her earlier objections. Arching with a low moan, she shoved a hand into his hair, pulling his mouth against her. Her suddenly overheated sex rippled as his tongue plunged in and began feasting on her with deep swirling licks.

"Mmm … you're so tasty Mrs Clarke…" Hugh growled, his tongue never ceasing in its exploration as he ate her hungrily. "I could eat your cunt all night."

His face was buried in her tender flesh, completely immersing him in her core as her cream flowed readily into his greedy mouth. She had a unique flavour, one he couldn't get enough of her and sucked her folds before working his tongue in and out, orally fucking her into delirium.

"Hugh … Oh fuck!" Elizabeth was on the verge of losing all control, her whole body was aquiver from the things his mouth was doing to her. Still sensitive from her self-induced climax, she knew it wouldn't be long before she reached her peak. Her thighs tightened instinctively, trying to hold him in place while she greedily bucked and ground her pelvis against him in a desperate attempt to make his tongue go as deep as possible.

This was something Patrick had never done for her. Though he expected it often, her loving husband never felt the need to return the favour. Hugh, however, was more than happy to attend to her, and oh God was he was so good at it. Already she could feel herself returning to the edge of that sweet precipice. Her hand clutched desperately at clumps of his hair as his tongue mercilessly pillaged her core, stretching to its limit and caressing her deeper than she'd ever thought possible. It felt like he was licking her everywhere at once.

Eager to give her what she craved, Hugh altered tactics and, with both arms coiled around her thighs, pivoted her up ever so slightly. In this new position, he was afforded greater access to her body and didn't wait before switching to suckle her clit.

"Oh, sweet Jesus … Hugh, please, please … I … I … oh my god, you're going to make me cum again … yes, yes, yes, oh fuck I'm gonna cum, I'm gonna…"

She thought she was going to die.

When he sucked her little bundle of nerves, a thousand different explosions went off in her head at once. Oh yes, she was going to die. She was going to burn up in the fires of her own ecstasy.

"Yeah, cum for me, Mrs Clarke," Hugh growled, staring up at her, his gaze dark and hot with lust. "You're so fucking sexy, feed me your wet cunt and cum on my face as I eat your pussy."

She looked so amazing like this, so dishevelled and uninhibited, so unlike the woman he had known while growing up.

Caught in his stare, Elizabeth couldn't look away. Even as the orgasm exploded through her, called up by his very command, she was possessed, rooted by the desire burning in his eyes, the sheer sensuality of watching him go down on her as waves rushed over her. They crested higher and higher, until the storm passed, and she was reduced to a panting mess.

Licking his lips clean, Hugh lowered her legs off of his shoulders and rose up to his full height between her drooping limbs. At some point he must have unfastened his trousers. They were open and his cock stood rampant between muscular thighs, the wide crest poised at her cleft. With a roll of his hips, he dragged the weeping tip along her folds to nudge her oversensitive clit.

The contact sent a thrill through Elizabeth that made her back arch. She wanted this. No, she needed this, but not here. Not in her kitchen.

"Take me to bed."

CHAPTER
6

Hugh Didn't question her decision. With a nod, he heaved her up and crushed her to him. Instinctively, she crossed her legs over his buttocks and swept her hands over his shoulders, scoring him lightly with her nails and marvelling at the wall of muscle beneath his shirt. He carried her effortlessly out of the kitchen, down the hall and up the stairs to the master bedroom.

He didn't bother turning on the light. Elizabeth was glad of that. The darkness helped her nervousness, made her feel like she was somewhere other than her family home, and it hid the photos. They were many- and everywhere. Photos of birthdays and events. Photos of her family and friends, of Victor. She didn't think she could do this with him watching.

However enough light was provided by the window for Hugh to discern the outline of the grand canopied king size bed. He made straight for it, but he didn't notice the rug at its foot. He slipped and they tumbled together onto the neatly made covers with Elizabeth on top.

She felt a thrill shiver down her spine as she took in the sight of the young man lying beneath her, unable to keep the devious smirk from her lips.

Strong, intelligent, and handsome, there wasn't a red-blooded woman alive that wouldn't give her right arm just to have him look at them the way he was at her. And yet, at this moment, he only had eyes for her, the mother of his best friend. A middle-aged housewife who had given the best years of her life to a neglectful, drunkard and adulterer. What had she ever done to get so lucky?

Smirking wickedly, Elizabeth winked, then shuffled her butt back down his legs.

Hugh gave her a quizzical look. "Mrs Clarke?"

"I love it when you call me that," she purred, keeping her eyes locked to his until she found what she was looking for and gave a surprised gasp. "Wow, you've grown into such a *big boy*."

Then, with her eyes still burning into his, she dipped her head and dragged the flat of her tongue up the underside of his cock from root to tip before going to work on him.

Hugh groaned and fisted the sheets, unable to look away as she bowed her head, those full pink lips stretched tight and gliding down his cock, sucking him in.

"Oh fuck, Mrs Clarke…"

Whenever he called her that, it just sounded so dirty. Elizabeth couldn't help moaning around her mouthful. And he was a mouthful. She'd wanted to take him all in, but he was much too big for that. Only a third of the way down and she was already at her limit. Yet that only made her feel naughtier. He just smelled so good, and his taste- she'd never known a man could taste so good. Pulling back, her cheeks hollowed as she sucked and mouthed his thick crown.

"Is this what you want Hugh, your best friend's mum sucking your cock?"

Releasing the head, she swirled her tongue around and around the wide crest, pulling back to tease the tip with flicking licks, before dragging the flat of her tongue up and down his length. And all the while still looking up into his eyes.

"Mmm … such a yummy cock, I bet you make all the girls choke with this big dick…"

It was too much. Hugh couldn't take it.

"Oh shit!" he groaned, eyes rolling up and his head falling back into the bed's soft embrace.

Elizabeth grinned inwardly, relishing the feeling of his cock pulsing under her tongue. "I want it, you bad boy, wanna feel this big dick splitting me open. I need it!"

Quick as a snake, Hugh lurched up, seized her around the waist and hurled her to the bed. Then, looming above her, he pulled his shirt over his head. With a flick of his wrist, he cast it aside. His shoes and trousers were gone just as quickly, leaving him standing before her in all his naked glory, the weak light glittering over his sculpted muscles and casting him in a godly radiance.

She didn't have time to enjoy the view, however. In the blink of an eye he was on top of her. With a quick tug, he had her robe undone and over her head. She gasped at his sudden ferocity, his new dominance a complete turn on that had her all but panting as the weight of his erection settled against her throbbing clit.

"Ready?"

"Yes!" Elizabeth wanted to scream. What was he waiting for? Couldn't he see that she'd never been more ready for anything in all her life. "Yes, damn it, just fuck me you bast-oh!"

Her back arched as her whole world was consumed in the delicious burn of his cock driving home. He filled her so completely, she could feel his every ridge and thick ropy vein coiled about his trunk. It was such a delicious sensation, she couldn't help fisting the sheets as her long legs closed around the sexy V-line of his waist and dug her heels into his flanks, urging him on.

Yet Hugh held firm. He had to.

Fuck, she felt so good. All hot, slick and so fucking snug. It was almost unbearable. It was only through force of sheer will that he was able to tear himself down from the edge before it was too late. Then her lush inner walls wrapped around him, squeezing his dick like a fist in a warm velvet glove, and it was too much.

He had to move.

"Oh god, oh shit … oh fuck!" Elizabeth felt ready to burst as Hugh started rolling his hips, drawing back then driving home, going deliciously deep as the flair of his hips spread her legs back. His pace was intolerably slow, but with each fervent drive she could feel herself opening to him, her delicate tissues stretching around every delicious inch of him. It was so raw, so intense.

Sex with her husband was nothing compared to this. Even the way he was looking at her. Patrick had never looked at her that way. He didn't want to possess her, to own and use her as though she were property. He wanted simply to love her, to be with her in every way that two people could be. The way nobody had ever been with her before.

This wasn't just lust or longing, this was something more, something deeper. Something both sacred and beautiful.

Elizabeth couldn't stand it. "Oh god, I'm cumming"

"That's it, cum for me, *Mrs Clarke*." His command was a low growl in her ear before he kissed her, smashing his mouth to hers, his tongue stroking hers as she came.

Shaking, riding the waves, Elizabeth clung to him, hands grabbing and clawing every bit of him she could reach, barely able to hang on. Desperate for more, she moved with him, grinding against each lunge of his big dick even as they sent her spiralling higher and higher.

Feeling her writhe under him, Hugh was certain he was orbiting madness.

It took all of his will not to give into his dark side, his primitive side. The debased animal that lurked in the heart of every man. The beast that yearned to take this woman, to make her beg and scream his name. It clawed at his resolve, whispering a sweet song of dominance and mastery. Yet he wanted this to be more than just fucking.

Now was his chance to show her, to prove to her, that there was more for her than just the mundane existence of a lonely housewife for her. That he was a better man than her good-for-nothing husband. His time had come and hooking an arm round her waist, he pulled her close, driving her hot little cunt all the way down to his root, as he reared back and pushed up onto his knees.

"Oh God!" Elizabeth gasped, ripping her lips from his in a long moan as his new angle of penetration scraped her sweet spot just right.

The way he held her had her hips pinned to his and as he rocked back and forth, her clit was dragged deliciously against his abdomen. The sensation was so intense, it made her head spin. Completely absorbed in her own pleasure, her lips had formed an 'O' shape and with each jolting thrust, her whole body jumped delightedly to meet him, causing her enchantingly full breasts to bounce. "Yes, yes, yes! Harder baby! Please … fuck me harder!"

"Yeah, ride my dick Mrs Clarke, ride it!"

"Oh my god… so much… so deep…oh fuck… it's amazing!" She was shaking again, her whole body humming as waves of sensation washed through her and goose bumps rose up all over her skin.

"You love my cock, don't you?"

"Yes! I love it, fuck my pussy more, I want it, I love it"

"Is it better than your husband's?"

To emphasise his question, he buried himself in her warmth again and saw the dam inside her crack beneath a sudden mini climax that caused her eyes to roll. Her body began to tremble as liquid ecstasy rushed through her and Hugh watched with unabashed delight, fucking her through the pleasure with quick stabs of his cock.

"So … so much better, oh fuck. I had no idea what I've been missing … I … I never knew sex could be so … so good! Fuck me more, make me take it, use me like he never cou-oh!" The cry left her lips before her mind could register what she had said, yet it was too late. Her body was melting in a sea of liquid pleasure and all sense of words and thought had left her. Moaning hotly as she tossed her head from side to side, her sweat dampened mane of raven hair fanning out around her, she caught only the briefest glimpse of him smirking down at her. It was a very hot look on him. It made the throbbing knot in her centre pulse dangerously, pushing her towards her pleasure's violent pinnacle.

"And who is the best fuck of your life?" Perspiration glistened across his bronzed skin and a few salty drops rolled down his neck as he felt himself nearing his limit.

"You! Oh Fuck … you Hugh … it … oh god, yes … it was always you … so good … I can't take it … I'm … I'm cumming!"

Even as she spoke, she could feel her arms coiling around his neck as her arse began to gyrate in his lap. They were so close now her every gasping breath was perfumed with his musky scent and she was suddenly aware of how hot his skin felt against her body. The sensations were so intense, her world had dissolved into a brilliant rush of colour and she couldn't tell where one tide of pleasure ceased and the next began as they merged into one continuous flood of glorious ecstasy. Was she going mad?

Or perhaps this was what it felt like to die?

Maybe death by sex wasn't just some delightful male fantasy and this terrific young stud had indeed fucked her into an early grave.

"Yeah, that's it, cum for me Mrs Clarke, cum all over my … my- oh fuck! I'm cumming too!"

The visual stimuli of her gorgeous naked body writhing and wriggling atop his pillaging shaft, combined with the feel of her juices coating him as her walls closed tight, sent him over the edge. After being restrained for so long, the force of his release was like nothing he had ever experienced, and a thunderous groan bellowed from his lips as his seed surged into her womb.

Still joined in the most intimate of fashions, they collapsed together in a tangled mass of limbs on the bed, their chests heaving with laboured breaths. Sweat made their bodies glisten in the low light yet neither made any effort to move. Feeling safe and content in the others' presence, they fell into a blissful sleep.

Epilogue

*E*lizabeth didn't want to wake.

Usually she was an early riser and would be up with the sun. There were chores to do, breakfasts to make, and an ever-mounting list of jobs. Her jobs.

However, today she just couldn't bring herself to do it. It felt safe here, safe and warm. Here she felt at peace, content.

Light, so very bright with all the magnificence of the dawn, blanketed her naked body. Winter was coming, its frosty breath wafted through the window, caressing her skin with soft and tantalising fingers fragrant with all the flavours of Autumn.

Half asleep, she trembled as the air teased down her back and arms, stirring goose flesh, and it was only when arms, strong as oak and corded with muscle, coiled around her waist, pulling her back against the wall of hard male lying beside her that she settled.

Satisfied to just lie back and enjoy the moment, Elizabeth made no effort to resist as he crushed her to him, a soft moan escaping her as her breasts were pressed into his chiselled torso and the weight of his cock rose up to nestle in the cradle of her thighs. It was such a delectable sensation. The feeling of his hands around her *and breath hot on her neck, the deep rhythmic drumming of his heart, the heat radiating off his body, enveloping her, dragging her back down into sweet serenity.*

And she couldn't remember ever feeling so sated.

Despite it all, she fought against the urge to curl into him, to sleep and prolong the moment across the boundless seas of eternity. Taken instead by the sudden need to see him, and an irrational fear that it might have all been a dream. A hot, wonderful, sweaty dream.

The greatest fucking dream of my life.

Just the memory of it stoked the embers in her core to new life. Suddenly more awake than asleep, she peeled her eyes back slowly to meet the stormy grey-blue eyes watching her from beneath sandy sleep-tousled hair.

"Mmm ... good morning," he purred, in a smoky voice that made her whole body tighten. Or maybe it was the way his mouth moved over the words, slow and seductive, pronouncing each syllable with delicious purpose. He had a very nice mouth. Thin peach coloured lips perfectly shaped with a sexy indent in the corner from where he had frequently bitten them when he was concentrating. A mouth made for kissing, licking and doing the most wicked things. And that jaw, like an anvil with the perfect amount of rough to tease her inner thighs when he was tonguing her clit.

She couldn't help blushing at the memory, the heat in her core spreading out in a scarlet flush as she averted her gaze.

No one had ever looked at her the way he had just then. It was so intense, so intimate. Much too intimate. Like he was seeing her, truly seeing her. Seeing more than the neglected married woman in desperate need of a good shag. More than just Victor's mother. More than...

She couldn't bear it. "No."

"What?" he smirked, pulling her closer, practically skin to skin. He was hard, like chiselled stone, but they fit together perfectly. A carved marble Adonis shaped just for her.

"Don't look at me like that … it's embarrassing."

"I can't help it. Mmm … that blush is just so sexy." He dipped his head to nip the curve of her neck, his tongue quick to sooth the delicious hurt.

"No … please … you can't, I'm still sore- oh!" She gasped when he scraped that sweet spot behind her ear, her eyes rolling. His hand came up to knead her breast, thumb and forefinger rolling her nipple so roughly she couldn't help arching into his palm.

"Mmm … you have amazing tits."

Tonguing the shell of her ear, Hugh seized upon Elizabeth's momentary distraction to push her back down onto the bed, caging her glorious naked body with his before taking a nipple into his mouth. He sucked greedily, and the delicious cocktail of heat and suction around her sensitive nub had her back arching, her fingers fisting his sandy strands.

"Oh god … mmm…" she moaned, clutching his head to her breast as the fog of pleasure descended.

Damn him!

Why did he have to be so good? How was she supposed to resist this young stud when just the feel of his mouth on her breast was enough to make her loins throb with liquid passion?

"I…can't…oh god! Stick it in…fuck me! Fuck me with your big dick!"

Hugh, however, was in no hurry.

Licking the tip of her nipple, he slowly reached between her quivering thighs and slid a finger along her wet sex while gently circling her clit with his thumb. Low sounds flowed from her in heated breaths as her hips rolled wantonly against his touch. And taking that as his cue, he suddenly snapped her legs open. Hearing her surprised squeak, he grinned wolfishly around her breast before moving into position, the rounded crest of his cock sliding up and down her folds…

The sound rang out as loud and shrill as a banshee's wail.

Lost in the depths of her fantasy, it hit Elizabeth like a bucket of ice water.

Atop the bedside table, the digital clock was flashing, illuminating the time in bright red numerals. Its alarm sang its ear-splitting song.

Besides her, Patrick lurched awake.

"Oh shit, I'm late!" he barked, jumping up from the bed and gathering up his clothes from the floor.

Tangled in the bed's voluminous sheets, Elizabeth watched as her husband pulled his trousers up doughy legs and shoved his shirt down a waistband that visibly strained to contain his suety bulk before waddling out their bedroom.

Downstairs, the front door slammed shut behind him. His Alfa's V12 engine roared to life, its tires squealed and there was a blast of a protesting neighbour's horn as he sped off down the street.

With a sigh, Elizabeth rolled over and silenced the cursed clock before falling back into the mound of pillows.

He didn't spare her so much as a backwards glance.

So, what else is new.

It was the same every time he had to go away on a sales trip. She'd like to say she was used to it, but the idea that he could just up and leave her without even saying goodbye left a very bitter taste in the back of her throat.

Had he ever even loved her? Had there ever been a chance for them?

Hot tears began to well at the corners of her eyes.

No, I won't cry! She told herself. *I won't cry for him. He's not worth it.*

For what felt like hours, Elizabeth toyed with the idea of going back to sleep. However, her body was trembling with unspent passion and before long the burning in her loins, that constant reminder of how close she'd come, drove her from her bed. Letting the sheets fall to the floor, she quickly donned her fluffy pink dressing gown before walking down the steps that led up to and from the master bedroom. Going through the hall and into the kitchen, she busied herself for a moment with the task of making a strong cup of tea before walking out into the back garden and breathing in the cool morning air.

It was hard to believe it was already October. Her garden was as beautifully vibrant as it had been in spring. The trees were still green. Everywhere flowers bloomed. Birds sang.

Nothing was right and yet it was all so perfect. So much like her own life.

And now, for another week, she was free.

It had been a month since the night she had decided to change her life. A month since she had given into temptation, broken her marriage vows, and surrendered her body and soul.

A month since she had taken Hugh Becket as her lover. Hugh, the boy she'd watched growing up, the young lawyer just coming home after years of living in the city. Hugh, her son's best Friend.

And the greatest fuck of my life.

Something had happened to her that night. Something that went beyond mere sex. He'd opened her eyes to a whole new world, given her a glimpse of something new and exciting. Something she'd never dreamed she was capable of. She wanted to experience it.

Her son, her precious baby boy, was all grown up and away at university. Her husband was never at home. This was a new day, a new start and a new chapter of her life. She was free to find herself, to discover who she was. She would recreate herself, and she knew just where to start.

Going back into the house, she retrieved her brand-new laptop from its hideaway under the kitchen table and started it up. Entering the password that was guaranteed to be uncrackable, at least to her dear loving husband who hadn't remembered their anniversary once in all their years of marriage, she selected the pre-installed Word processor. The screen went white with the infamous white page.

What better way to reinvent herself than by creating her character in a book?

Sipping her tea, she considered the screen for a moment, then began to type.

Confessions of a Trophy Wife.

By Liz Becket

The End

ALSO BY
L.M. MOUNTFORD

TEMPTATION JUST GOT EVEN SWEETER...

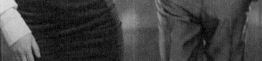

Sweet
Temptations:
THE BOSS'S DAUGHTER

THE LORD OF LUST
L.M. MOUNTFORD

Sweet Temptations:

THE BOSS'S DAUGHTER

He thought his temptations were over, but they were only just
beginning…

Until last week, Richard Martin was just another middle-aged
guy. Married to a wife he loved, father to a son he adored, stuck
in a dead-end job, just counting the days go by…

Then everything changed.

He made a mistake.

Now to save his marriage, he's going to have to pay the price.

There's just one problem, Scarlet Holmes.

His Supervisor.

She loves to play games with her staff and now, seeming very
aware of his little secret, she wants to play a game.

And she always gets what she wants.

Because she just so happens to be The Boss's Daughter.

Dom Diaries

Serving
THE SENATOR

L.M. MOUNTFORD

He is my Hades

I'd played the role of a goddess, bound and chained for the service of mortals.

He freed me.

He freed me, unchained me and taken me to his underworld, his dark realm where he'd brought out all my forbidden and secret desires.

And now I'm his.

His attendant. His servant…

Serving the Senator is a sizzling new release from the lord of Lust. Loaded with tension and sizzling chemistry, it is a modern reimagining of the ancient myth of Hades and Persephone. A stand-alone romance, it is loaded with scenes of an adult nature that feature BDSM, Dominance play, and so much heat, they may very well melt your e-reader…

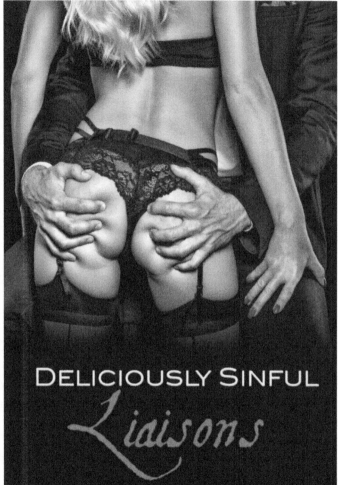

DELICIOUSLY SINFUL
Liaisons

A COLLECTION OF HOT AND ORGASMIC STORIES
FROM THE LORD OF LUST

L.M. MOUNTFORD

DELICIOUSLY SINFUL
Liaisons

A collection of hot and orgasmic stories by The Lord of Lust

Do you love hard men, strong women, sizzling chemistry and erotic scenes that make Fifty Shades of Grey look like five shades of beige?
Well, here you go...

7 Books, 7 hard and rugged men, 7 sizzling page turners that will have you devouring every word from start to finish...

And for the first time ever, an extract from the lord's long-awaited and much-anticipated sequel to his debut Sweet Temptations: The Boss's Daughter

Warning: The stories in this steamy collection are so intense and the scene so hot, they may cause your kindle to melt while reading...

Temptation
And
Seduction

L.M. MOUNTFORD

Temptation
And
Seduction

Five tales of Lust, desire & Temptation

L.M. Mountford, The Lord of Lust, brings you a collection of some of his hottest works. 5 of the sexiest stories ever released on Kindle & Ereader…

Plus, for the first time ever, read an extract from the long-awaited sequel to his debut –
Sweet Temptation: The Boss's Daughter

*** These stories contain descriptions of sexual content, Violence, BDSM, Paranormal, S&M & Dubious Consent for 18+ Adults only***

THEIR SILENCE COMES AT A PRICE...

UNCOVERED

THE LORD OF LUST

L.M. MOUNTFORD

UNCOVERED

L. M. MOUNTFORD

My stepbrother and I have always been close, sometimes we were VERY close.

It was our little secret, until his friends walked in on us. Now they know our secret and **they want to play too...**

When Mina returns for her stepbrother's 21st birthday, she thinks her days of lusting after him are over. Caught up in the heat and passion of the moment, she is stunned to find them back in bed together; their feelings clearly far from resolved.

Haunted by her desire, Mina now has another problem… she must head down a path of lust and desire; torn between the dark delights of the handsome bad boy down the street and her adorable stepbrother who has always been there for her. Can she confront the truth she has long tried to bury? How far will she go to save the one she wants, but knows she can never truly have?

A full length, 40,000+ word novel, Uncovered is the stand-alone erotic drama from the Author of the sinfully delicious, Sweet Temptations Trilogy. Warning! It contains adult themes, harsh language, and graphic content, descriptions of intense sexual scenes, and dubcon (dubious consent) that might be triggers for some readers.

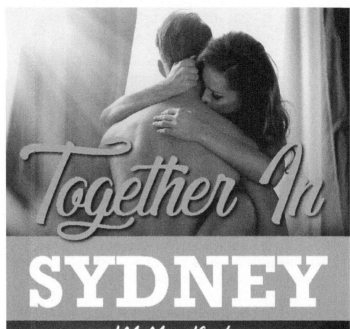

Together In

SYDNEY

LM Mountford

Together In

SYDNEY

LM Mountford

I may have been a bad influence on her when we were kids, but this new side of her is going to ruin me...

They were the best of friends. Then they shared a night of passion and in the morning she was gone and Alex has spent years trying to move on.

But then an email arrives out of the blue and suddenly he finds himself boarding the first plane bound for Australia with nothing but his passport and an overnight bag. He's no idea what he'll do, or he's going to say, but one thing's for sure...

He's not going home without her.

Together in Sydney is a Second Chance Romance full of steamy scenes and bad language. It's only recommended for readers 18+. No cliffhanger. Guaranteed HEA!

An erotic PNR/Vampire story by
LM Mountford

Blood
Lust

The Thirst always
wins...

Blood Lust

Sooner or later, the thirst always wins…

After a thousand years, Lucian had given up any interest in the world. His only concern that night was finding his next drink, preferably from a flavoursome twenty-something with loose morals and no expectations. Then he saw her…

Kate is just a girl from the country, who came to the city with her brother to find a life away from their parents' car crash. That is until the police came knocking on her door one morning and ripped her new life apart.

Now she has nothing and no one, with only one on her mind... When these worlds collide, and the things that go bump in the night come calling, can these two mend the rifts in each other and give them what they need?

__Blood Lust__ is a sizzling-hot Paranormal romance. If you like strong-willed, sassy heroines and oh-so-bad, drop-dead gorgeous Vampire heroes with lots of bite, you'll love this page turner.

TRAINING
Tracey

THEY'LL TEACH
THEIR DAUGHTER'S
BEST FRIEND A
LESSON SHE WILL
NEVER FORGET...

L.M. MOUNTFORD

TRAINING
Tracey

I know it's wrong to want my best friend's dad... but what about when his wife offers to share?

Tracey has known the Burtons practically all her life.
They're her best friend's parents.

When she was a little girl they took her on days out to the beach.
But she's a woman now, and they have some very important lessons to teach her...

** Training Tracey is A wicked and uber-hot coming-of-age menage, filled with MF, FF & MFF scenes from the Lord of Lust's Dark and Dirty alter ego. There is NO cheating, NO cliffhanger and a guaranteed HEA with plenty of steam. **

WARNING 18+: This book is erotic and contains material that may be considered offensive to some readers, which includes graphic language, explicit sex, and adult situations.

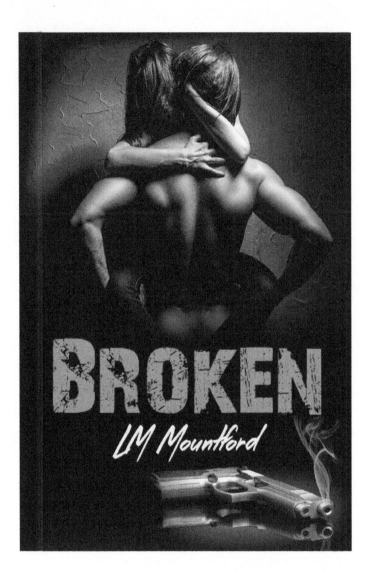

BROKEN

LM Mountford

BROKEN

Vickey Romano is the girl with a secret you don't want to bring home to mum.

Beautiful, haunted, and on the run, she works a string of temp jobs and never lets anyone get too close. Until that is, she meets Jake. The living definition of dark and dangerous, he tells her nothing about himself, keeps a SIG P226 in his bedside table and can make her go weak-kneed with just a word.

She knows she should stay away, he has her caught in his web and she's helpless to resist.

All she can do is hope her past doesn't kill him in the process...

Broken is a hard and gritty Dark romance. The opening in the Broken Heart Series, it balances sex and violence on a knife edge and will draw you down a web of mystery with every page.

PLAY TIME
BOOKS 1 & 2

Play Time: Double Period combines Naughty Students, Magic Girls & Demonic Succubus Teachers that will suck you dry and leave you begging for another round.

Here both the titillating Paranormal Erotica Hit and it's sequel, Extra Credit are available like never before in a 30,000+ word lesson in submission, BDSM and Fem Domination that will have you hooked page after page.

Made in the USA
Monee, IL
07 August 2022

11062536R00049